PANDORA'S
BOX

PANDORA'S BOX

Rose Impey

Illustrated by Peter Bailey

BLOOMSBURY EDUCATION

LONDON OXFORD NEW YORK NEW DELHI SYDNEY

BLOOMSBURY EDUCATION
Bloomsbury Publishing Plc
50 Bedford Square, London, WC1B 3DP, UK

BLOOMSBURY, BLOOMSBURY EDUCATION and the Diana logo
are trademarks of Bloomsbury Publishing Plc

First published in Great Britain in 2007 by A&C Black, an imprint
of Bloomsbury Publishing Plc

This edition published in 2020 by Bloomsbury Publishing Plc

Text copyright © Rose Impey, 2007
Illustrations copyright © Peter Bailey, 2007

Packaged for Bloomsbury by Plum5 Limited

Rose Impey and Peter Bailey have asserted their rights under the Copyright,
Designs and Patents Act, 1988, to be identified as Author and Illustrator of this work

A catalogue record for this book is available from the British Library

ISBN: PB: 978-1-4729-6746-6; ePDF: 978-1-4729-6745-9;
ePub: 978-1-4729-6747-3

2 4 6 8 10 9 7 5 3 1

Printed and bound by CPI Group (UK) Ltd, Croydon, CR0 4YY

CONTENTS

CHAPTER ONE

In the Beginning

Of all the gods in ancient Greece, Zeus was Top God. He ruled over the whole Earth from his home on Mount Olympus.

It was a beautiful world but there were no living creatures in it yet, so Zeus decided to make some.
He asked two other gods to help.

Epimetheus made the animals and birds and insects.

His brother, Prometheus, made the humans. They made them out of mud. Then they breathed life into them.

Now, when Prometheus created Man, he made him look like the gods and Zeus was very angry.

He wanted Man to worship the gods and always depend on them.

He did not want Man to think he was their equal.

"Listen to me," Zeus warned Prometheus. "You must not give Man any more powers!"

But Prometheus did not listen to Zeus. He loved Man and did not like seeing him shivering in the cold and rain.

If Man had fire, he would be warm, thought Prometheus, and he could cook food. Life would be so much easier for him.

In the dead of night, Prometheus crept to Mount Olympus and stole fire from the gods. Then he brought it back to Earth and gave it to Man.

When Zeus found out, he was beyond anger.

"I am god of all gods!" he raged. "Man will suffer for this. And you, Prometheus, for disobeying me, will suffer most of all."

Zeus was a fierce, harsh god. When he took his revenge that was harsh, too.

He chained Prometheus to a
rock on a mountain top, and left
him to be pecked at by eagles, day
and night.

Because gods never die, this
punishment would last for ever
and ever. Prometheus had no hope
of escape.

But Zeus did not stop there.
Next he planned to teach Man
a lesson he would never forget.

CHAPTER TWO
The Gift

As part of his plan, Zeus decided to make the first woman. Again he asked the other gods for help.

He told them to give Woman many talents: such as creativity, wit and mastery of language.

He told them to make her clever
and graceful and full of compassion.
and she became all of those things.

Zeus said, "I shall call her
Pandora, meaning full of talents."
Then he sent for Epimetheus.

"I have made a woman to live on Earth with you," he told him, smiling through his teeth. "I hope you will both be very happy."

Prometheus had warned his brother never to trust Zeus. But Epimetheus didn't suspect a thing. As soon as he and Pandora met they fell in love and in no time they were married.

All the gods sent wedding
presents. Zeus sent a large wooden
chest with carvings all over it.
A large label that said: DO NOT
OPEN was attached to the top.

"What is the point of a present you cannot open?" said Pandora. "Surely we could just peep inside?"

But Epimetheus had not forgotten what had happened to his brother.

"We do not want to disobey the gods," he said.

He took the box and put it in
a far corner of the house.

Then he hid it under a cloth.

Out of sight, out of mind,
he told himself.

Besides, Epimetheus did not feel
that he needed presents. He had
Pandora who seemed like a goddess
to him.

But she wasn't a goddess, Zeus had made sure of that. He had told the gods that as well as her many talents Woman must have the trait of curiosity.

The box *may* have been out of sight, but it was *not* out of Pandora's mind.

CHAPTER THREE

Before the Box

At first, life for Epimetheus and Pandora seemed perfect. He was kind and loving and, with all her many talents, Pandora made a wonderful wife for him.

In every way, Epimetheus was completely happy.

But Pandora was not. When she was alone in the house, there was often something at the back of her mind, poking and prodding her.

"I hope you haven't forgotten about me!" a little voice would whisper. "I am still there – in the corner – waiting."

Pandora tried to ignore the voice. "Who cares about the stupid box?" she said.

She tried to tell herself she was not interested.

She even tried to pretend it did not exist.

But some people, when they're told they *must not* do something, simply *have to* do it.

Pandora was one of those people.

The harder she tried to put the box out of her mind, the more she thought about it. Soon she could think of nothing else.

Over and over again, she found herself standing right in front of it.

"I don't know how that happened," she would say, surprised. Then, wisely, she would walk away.

But one day Pandora did not walk away. She made sure she was all alone. Then she told herself, "It can't hurt to have just one little look."

Pandora reached out to touch the box, but then she stopped herself.

"What would Epimetheus say?" she asked out loud.

"Epimetheus does not need to know," the voice answered her. "It can be your secret, Pandora."

Pandora nodded. "After all," she reminded herself, "it *is* half my wedding present."

She knelt down. Very gently she removed the cloth. Then a strange thing happened...

Pandora could hear noises coming from the box. It sounded as if something – or lots of things – might be trapped inside, trying to get out.

CHAPTER FOUR
The Damage is Done

Pandora knew she should not open the box. But now her curiosity had completely taken over.

What was inside?

What could be making those noises?

Was it something *alive*?

"I'll just take a quick peep," she told herself. "And then I'll lock it up."

Then a different voice – a sensible one – inside her head said: "Walk away, Pandora. Leave the box alone."

And she almost did. But the noises called her back. It was no use. Pandora knew she would not be able to rest until she had opened that lid.

As she began to turn the key, the noises grew louder. It was as if hundreds of tiny insects were hissing in her ear, "Hurry up, Pandora! Don't stop now!"

For a moment, Pandora felt scared and almost stopped...

But by now she was bursting to find out what was inside.

She lifted the lid, only a crack…

Within seconds, hundreds of
horrible things swarmed out,
like bees from a hive.

There were creepy-crawling things, sweaty-swarming things, scary-scratching things, buzzing and biting things, all flying around her head.

The air was thick with them as they brushed against her face.

"Ugh! Get away! Get away!" she shouted, waving her arms about.

Pandora tried to close the lid, but it would not go back on the box. She tried to sit on it, but it sprang open and tipped her onto the floor.

More and more things poured out, surrounding her.

"Stop! Stop!" she begged.
"I'm sorry. I didn't mean to do it!"
But the things went on hissing
and buzzing until the noise almost
deafened her.

Just when Pandora thought she
could not bear it any more,
the things stopped buzzing
and poured smoke-like
through the open
window.

Soon they were all gone, out into the world, spreading their horrible powers into every corner.

CHAPTER FIVE
The Last Chance

Pandora knew she had done
something bad. But she did not
realise *how* bad. She did not know
with what kind of horrors Zeus
had filled the box.

Until then, no one on Earth
had ever been ill, or afraid, or
greedy, or jealous. No one had
been unkind to anyone else.

War did not exist. Until then,
no one had even died. The world
had been free of all those troubles.

Now Pandora had let them out.

This was the punishment Zeus had created for Man.

Pandora could only stand and watch as the sky turned dark and heavy, and a cold, cold wind blew into the room. She shivered and turned back to the box. She tried again to close the lid.

Then she noticed something left in the corner, a pale, fragile thing, and it did not hiss or buzz.

Instead, it whispered, "Do not leave me in here."

But Pandora said, "Oh, no. At least I can make sure one of you does not escape." And she almost closed the lid.

"Please wait!" it begged. "This is your chance to put things right. I am Hope; you must let me out, too."

Pandora wanted to believe that even now it was not too late and so she did as it asked. She opened the lid wide and watched the small scrap of Hope fly out. For a moment it lit up the whole room.

Then it followed the others through the open window and out into the world. A thin ray of sunshine broke through the dark cloud. Pandora stopped shivering and suddenly felt less scared.

Chained to his rock, Prometheus heard the first sounds of pain and suffering across the Earth. He wondered how Man would deal with the horrors that were now loose in the world, without him there to protect them.

Just then a pale, fragile creature flew past. Prometheus saw that it was Hope. For the first time, he believed that one day Zeus might set him free. He began to think of better things to come.

Look out for more books in the
BLOOMSBURY READERS SERIES

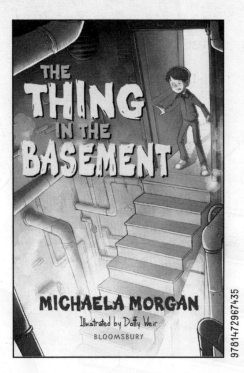

THE
THING
IN THE
BASEMENT

MICHAELA MORGAN

Illustrated by Daffy Weir

BLOOMSBURY

9781472967435

As Scott passes the basement steps on his
first day at his new school, there's a bang
and a flash and a roaring sound. Scott knows
there's something down there. Something nasty.
Something dangerous...

Look out for more books in the
BLOOMSBURY READERS SERIES

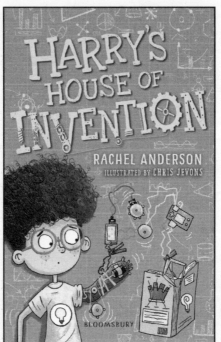

Harry's mum is an inventor who makes strange machines. His dad is a chef who invents new recipes. Life is almost perfect until Harry breaks his arm. Luckily his mum has a new invention for him to try out...

Look out for more books in the
BLOOMSBURY READERS SERIES

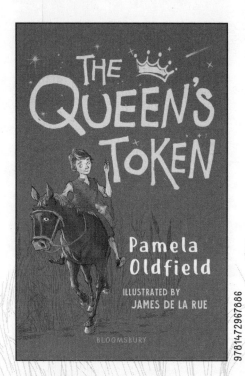

Hal is a stable boy with a dream – to work for
King Henry VIII. But when he meets the royal
party by chance he gets mistaken for a spy and
soon his fate rests in the hands of the king.
Will King Henry live up to his fierce reputation?